THIS BOOK
BELONGS TO

PEANUTS®
A Charlie Brown
VALENTINE

By Charles M. Schulz
Based on the animated special, the text was adapted by Natalie Shaw
Illustrated by Robert Pope

Simon Spotlight
New York London Toronto Sydney New Delhi

SIMON SPOTLIGHT
An imprint of Simon & Schuster Children's Publishing Division
1230 Avenue of the Americas, New York, New York 10020
This Simon Spotlight edition December 2016

SIMON SPOTLIGHT and colophon are registered trademarks of Simon & Schuster, Inc. For information about special discounts for bulk purchases, please contact Simon & Schuster Special Sales at 1-866-506-1949 or business@simonandschuster.com. Manufactured in the United States 1117 OPM
10 9 8 7 6 5 4   ISBN 978-1-4814-6803-9   ISBN 978-1-4814-6804-6 (eBook)

Valentine's Day is around the corner! Charlie Brown and his friends are busy preparing for the big day . . . and hoping to receive valentines of their own. "Valentine's Day puzzles me, Chuck," Peppermint Patty confides in him. "If someone gives you a great big valentine, does that mean they love you?"

Charlie Brown thinks for a moment. "I don't think the size of the card really matters," he replies.

Peppermint Patty looks confused. "Have you received a lot of Valentine's Day cards?" she asks.

"Not even *one*," Charlie Brown admits, "but I have a feeling this will be the year!"

Just then Snoopy walks by with a wheelbarrow full of valentines.

Good grief, thinks Charlie Brown.

For Charlie Brown, Valentine's Day is just like any other day. As usual, he has a particular special someone on his mind.

"I'd give *anything* to be able to talk to that Little Red-Haired Girl," he says to himself at lunch as she walks by. "The amazing thing is, I *know* I'm the kind of person she would like. I'm not the greatest person who ever lived, of course, but who is?"

It turns out someone *does* think Charlie Brown is special . . . Marcie! She is making a valentine for him. When her friend Peppermint Patty finds out, she is surprised. "You can't do that! He'll think you like him!" Peppermint Patty tells Marcie. "I do! I'm very fond of Charles," Marcie replies.
That's when Peppermint Patty realizes she likes Charlie Brown too.

After school, Marcie walks to Charlie Brown's house and asks him an important question. "I may or may not be sending you a valentine, Charles, so I need to know something. Do you like me?" Marcie asks.

"Do I *what*?" Charlie Brown says, not really listening. "What?"

"Forget it," Marcie tells him.

Marcie tells Peppermint Patty she isn't giving a valentine to Charlie Brown after all. The next day, Peppermint Patty walks home with Charlie Brown and stands by as he checks the mailbox. When he sees an envelope inside with his name on it, his face lights up!

"Got a letter, eh, Chuck?" Peppermint Patty asks him, smiling.

Charlie Brown reads it aloud, "'I know you like me, and in my own way, I like you too!'"

Then he turns to Peppermint Patty and says excitedly, "I think it's from that Little Red-Haired Girl!"

Peppermint Patty scowls. "That letter is from me. You like *me*, Chuck!" she insists.

"I do?" Charlie Brown asks. He doesn't want to hurt her feelings, but he really thought the Little Red-Haired Girl sent him a valentine. *I guess it is too good to be true*, he thinks.

Charlie Brown can't help it: His heart belongs to the Little Red-Haired Girl.
He is determined to find the courage to give her a valentine, so he makes a
card and shows it to Sally and Snoopy.

Sally is worried. "What if she laughs in your face?" she asks her big brother.
Charlie Brown sighs. "At least I'd be near her."

Charlie Brown asks Snoopy to help him practice delivering the card. Charlie Brown goes outside their house, holds out the valentine, and rings the doorbell.

Snoopy comes out . . . wearing a bright red wig! He isn't much help, so Charlie Brown sets off for the Little Red-Haired Girl's house, rehearsing his speech on the way.

"Here, sweet Little Red-Haired-Girl. . . . I made this valentine for you," Charlie Brown says as he walks. Then he gulps and begins again. "Here, I hope you like this valentine as much as . . . as I like you!" He tries out a few different smiles and even a wink, but he is too nervous! When he spots a mailbox, he quickly drops the valentine inside without even signing his name on the card.

Next, Charlie Brown decides to buy some candy for the Little Red-Haired Girl. "I'd like to buy a box of candy for a girl who doesn't know I exist," he confesses to the candy-store clerk. "But nothing too expensive, ma'am. I'll never have the nerve to give it to her, anyway!"

Charlie Brown makes it all the way to the Little Red-Haired Girl's house . . . before stopping at a tree near her front door, too afraid to move closer.

Maybe I can hide behind this tree and hold out this box of candy, he thinks. *And when she comes by, she'll take it out of my hand.* He gets as far as hiding behind the tree and holding out the candy before realizing how silly he looks and heading home.

Then Charlie Brown gets the idea to invite the Little Red-Haired Girl to the school's Valentine's Day dance, but he asks Linus to find out if she likes him first.

"He sits across the room from you," Charlie Brown overhears Linus saying to the Little Red-Haired Girl. "By the window . . . no, in the last row . . . well, sort of a round face . . . no, 'brown,' like in 'town.'"

She doesn't even know who Charlie Brown is!

Finally, Lucy tells Charlie Brown to just walk up to the Little Red-Haired Girl and introduce himself.

"I can't talk to her!" Charlie Brown blurts out. "She has a pretty face, and pretty faces make me nervous."

Lucy is furious. "How come *my* face doesn't make you nervous, huh? I have a pretty face! How come you can talk to *me*?"

So Charlie Brown runs away and decides to ask Sally to deliver a note since he had trouble before. He hides as Sally rings the doorbell.

Will she laugh? Or can she possibly like me too? he wonders.

Then Sally returns, hands back the note, and shrugs. "She couldn't read your smudgy writing."

"I can't stand it!" Charlie Brown sighs.

At school, Linus urges Charlie Brown to seize the moment. "Ask her right now!"

Charlie Brown is too scared. "She's something, and I'm nothing," he explains. "If I were something and she were nothing, I could talk to her. Or if she were something and I were something. Or if she were nothing and I were nothing—"

"You know, Charlie Brown, for a nothing, you're really something!" Linus says.

On Valentine's Day, Charlie Brown and Snoopy get all dressed up and head to school for the dance.

"Dogs can't come in!" says the boy at the door.

"This kid thought it was a costume ball, so he wore a dog suit," Charlie Brown explains.

It works! Soon they are on the dance floor, and Charlie Brown spots the Little Red-Haired Girl.

"She's just waiting for you to ask her to dance," Linus says. "Go on!"
Charlie Brown's knees are shaking. His heart is pounding. He takes one step
and then another. "I'm going to ask her. . . . I'm getting there. . . . I'm . . ."
That's when Peppermint Patty and Marcie pull him onto the dance floor.
"You sly devil!" says Peppermint Patty. "We've been looking for you!"

Soon it's time for the last dance . . . but the Little-Red Haired Girl is already dancing with Snoopy!

"Good grief!" Charlie Brown sighs, realizing that was his last chance. Then he has a happy thought.

"Linus, maybe she sent me a valentine, but it was delayed in the mail. Maybe it's in the mailbox right now—a real fancy valentine with lace!"
So the next morning, Charlie Brown opens the mailbox . . .

. . . and Snoopy pops out and gives him a big kiss!

Snoopy hops to the ground and starts dancing. Then Charlie Brown and Linus are dancing too! Charlie Brown is disappointed that the Little Red-Haired Girl didn't send him a valentine, but he is happy to have such good friends. *Besides, there's always next year,* he thinks.

It is a very happy Valentine's Day after all!